MY HEADTEACHER IS A VAMPIRE RAT!

PAMELA BUTCHART

nosy crow

Look out for:

THE
SPY
WHO
LOVED
SCHOOL
DINNERS

BABY
ALIENS
GOT MY
TEACHER!

ATTACK
OF THE
DEMON
DINNER
LADIES

TO
WEE
OR
NOT TO
WEE!

THERE'S
A
WEREWOLF
IN MY
TENT!

First published in the UK in 2015 by Nosy Crow Ltd
The Crow's Nest, 14 Baden Place, Crosby Row
London, SE1 1YW, UK

Nosy Crow and associated logos are trademarks and/or registered
trademarks of Nosy Crow Ltd

Text copyright © Pamela Butchart, 2015
Cover and illustrations copyright © Thomas Flintham, 2015

The right of Pamela Butchart and Thomas Flintham to be identified
as the author and illustrator respectively of this work has been asserted
by them in accordance with the Copyright, Designs
and Patents Act 1988.

10

A CIP catalogue record for this book will be available from the British Library.

Printed and bound in the UK by Clays Ltd, St. Ives Plc

Papers used by Nosy Crow are made from wood grown in
sustainable forests.

ISBN: 978 0 85763 289 0

www.nosycrow.com

Contents

1. The Scariest Time EVER   1
2. BEWARE! DANGER! NO ENTRY!   8
3. Rat Bag   31
4. Classroom Chaos   38
5. Get Us Out Of Here!!!   50
6. The Cape   60
7. Traumatic Brains   73
8. Lies, Blood and Strawberry Milkshake   82
9. Rat Poo Shoe   100
10. Give Us Garlic Bread   107
11. The Biggest Pencil in the World   123
12. Evacuated   139
13. Garlic Muffins   151
14. Moth Jar Spy   164
15. Dogs, Rabies and Recycling Bins   181
16. He's Burning!   191
17. MEGA Trouble   198

18. Sorry For Melting Your Face   211
19. Who Hissed?!   234
20. Mary   245
21. We Love You Scary Mary   257

The Scariest Time EVER

I used to think that ghosts were the scariest things **EVER!** At our school we even have our own ghost, and she haunts the school dinners because that's where she died a hundred years ago when

1

she choked to death on the shepherd's pie.
And now she haunts the dinner hall and the
dinner ladies, but they still make shepherd's

pie. So I suppose she must not be that good
at haunting people.

Most people think it's only houses, and
castles and schools that can be haunted but
it's not; ANYTHING can be haunted. For

example, you could have a haunted shoe on right now and you wouldn't even know it. And there's not really any way to know for sure until your shoe flies off your foot or something. And then you know.

One time me and Jodi (that's my friend) found out that loads of stuff can be haunted when we were staying in a caravan with Jodi's gran, and Jodi's gran was sleeping, and Jodi was bored so she said, "Caravans are boring," and then all of a sudden Jodi's fold-away bed folded up with her inside it!

And I had to pull her out and it took ages because Jodi was tangled up in all the sheets

and she kept screaming,
"IT SMELLS IN HERE!
GET ME OUT!"

And then the next morning the toaster burned Jodi's toast. Then when Jodi was having a shower the water kept going hot then cold, then cold then hot, and Jodi kept screaming, and we both knew that the caravan ghost was annoyed at her because she'd said that caravans were boring. And it was obvious because all of the stuff was only happening to Jodi and not me, and not to her gran.

But this isn't the story about the Caravan Ghost, or about the Shepherd's Pie Ghost, or even about any ghosts at all. This is the story about the time that the weirdest and scariest

thing EVER happened. And it happened at our school. And it was even scarier than all the ghosts in the world coming to your house at the same time!

It was the

SCARIEST

time ever because it had to do with hundreds of vampire rats, and garlic muffins, and our other friend, Zach, nearly getting his nose blood drunk by the new Head Teacher!

And like Jodi says, when we broke into the Head Teacher's office to get the coffin we could have all been eaten alive!

BEWARE!
DANGER!
NO ENTRY!

Everything started on Monday when me and my friend Zach, who lives downstairs, got to school.

We tried to meet Jodi and our other friend Maisie outside the classroom before class started, like we always do, but we couldn't

even get up the stairs to where our classroom
is because there was a big sign that said,

BEWARE!
DANGER!
NO ENTRY!
ALL PUPILS REPORT
TO ASSEMBLY HALL.

I didn't have a CLUE what was going on,
and why our classroom and the stairs were
now DANGEROUS, because they had been
fine on Friday when we left school. So me
and Zach went to the staff room and knocked

on the door and asked for Miss Jones (that's our teacher). But when we asked her about all the DANGER signs, she just told us to do what the sign said and to report to the assembly hall, so we did. But I was a bit annoyed because even though Miss Jones is nice and everything, she could have just told us what was going on because she was standing RIGHT THERE.

So anyway, when we got to the hall, everyone was saying loads of stuff like how the school was crumbling to the ground, and about how if the assembly didn't hurry up and start we would probably all be buried

to death. I was starting to get a bit worried, but then I saw Jodi and Maisie standing in the store cupboard at the back of the hall, waving at us to come over.

That's when Jodi explained that there had been an EARTHQUAKE in the night. And that it had only affected the school, obviously. And that me and Zach needed to stand under the store-cupboard doorframe with her and Maisie for when the AFTERSHOCK hit. And that if we didn't, all the bricks would fall on our heads and kill us.

And this is one of the reasons that I am very happy I am friends with Jodi, because she is very good at lots of stuff to do with

DISASTERS,
and EMERGENCIES,

and she's even made an

EMERGENCY PLAN

about what we would do if one of us got accidently locked in the classroom.

Like the time that happened to Gary Petrie when he was in the store cupboard tidying up because that was his punishment for licking Lynsey Perry's pencil case. But then when the bell went for lunch, Miss Jones and everybody else forgot all about him being in there, and we all left and Miss Jones locked the door.

Then when we got back to the classroom after our lunch, we saw that Gary Petrie had his face squashed up against the glass, and that he was crying. Miss Jones was trying to open the door, but she couldn't get her key in the lock because Gary Petrie had got loads of pens, and pencils, and a ruler stuck in there when he was trying to escape.

So Miss Jones told us all to wait while she ran off to get help. But Gary Petrie just kept crying and screaming through the door about how he was STARVING and about how he needed a wee.

So me and Zach tried to squash half a Mars

Bar under the door, because even though I do not like Gary Petrie very much, because he does things like lick people's pencil cases and has bogey fingers, I still did not want him to starve to death.

So Gary Petrie ate a bit of the Mars Bar off the floor, and we asked him if he was feeling any better, and he said that he was worse, and that he was going to wee himself. And then he started panicking, and jumping around.

That's when Jodi said, "Gary. Listen to me very closely. You're going to have to do a wee in the bin."

Everyone was shocked. But then Jodi said that it was either that or Gary Petrie's bladder would explode and then he'd die. Then Jodi put her hand against the glass. And then Gary put his hand against the glass too. And

I knew it was because Jodi was trying to make Gary Petrie be brave.

Then Jodi told him that we would all go down to the end of the corridor so that we wouldn't see him doing a wee in the bin. And he said OK. And also that he didn't want to die. So we all ran down to the very end of the corridor and waited.

But then Miss Jones came back with the caretaker, and even though we all told her NOT to go up to the door, she went anyway. And that's when she screamed, and the caretaker said, "DISGRACEFUL BEHAVIOUR!" and nobody was allowed

back into the classroom until it had been completely DISINFECTED.

So anyway, we all stood under the doorframe, like Jodi had said to do, and waited for the assembly to start. Then Mrs Seith (the scary Deputy Head) appeared on stage, and she told everyone to "Calm down for goodness' sake!" and to "Sit on the floor and listen closely." So we all sat down, but we made sure that we were still under the doorframe.

And that's when I said, "Where's Mr Murphy?" because Mr Murphy is our Head Teacher, and he's usually on stage for ALL the assemblies.

But then Mrs Seith heard me talking **ALL THE WAY FROM THE STAGE** because she hears **EVERYTHING**. Like the time she told me and Zach off for running in the corridor, and we were at least a mile away from her because we'd seen her coming out of her office and we'd been worried that she'd found out about the Garden Gnome Incident (which I don't really have time to tell you about just now). So anyway, we were about a mile away from her, because we'd been running our fastest, and I

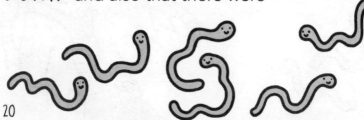

whispered, "Do you think she knows?" and that's when Mrs Seith shouted, "Do you think she knows **WHAT**, Isabella?" And I couldn't believe it! And to this day I still don't know how she heard me.

So anyway, I stopped talking **RIGHT AWAY** because Mrs Seith is **SERIOUSLY SCARY** and I didn't want her to shout at me in the assembly hall in front of all the Year 6s.

So we all listened to Mrs Seith do the assembly, and that's when she said that there had been **"NO EARTHQUAKE"** and that the school was definitely **"NOT FALLING DOWN"** and also that there were

"ABSOLUTELY
NO POISONOUS
CHAIR-EATING WORMS
WHATSOEVER ON
SCHOOL PREMISES".

And as soon as she
said the word "worm"
Maisie squealed,
because Maisie is
TERRIFIED OF
EVERYTHING,
and that includes

21

worms, and she usually just faints if you even say the word **"WORM"** never mind a poisonous one that eats chairs!

Then when Mrs Seith had finished staring at us for the squeal, she told us all that the reason for the

"DANGER! STAY OUT!"

signs was because the school roof was **LEAKING**, and that some parts of the school would be closed until the leaks in the roof had been fixed.

Then Mrs Seith started to tell us which

parts of the school were strictly "OUT OF BOUNDS" and we all listened closely. But then she said 4J, and WE are 4J! So that meant that OUR classroom was getting shut down, and we didn't know what was going to happen to us.

Zach smiled and said, "I bet we get to go home."

And Jodi said, "I bet we don't."

And then Mrs Seith said something that we couldn't believe. She said, "4J will be sharing a classroom with 6B." And then everyone in 6B groaned and looked at everyone in 4J because 6B are mostly horrible, and

they treat us like we're babies even though they're supposed to be nice to us because they're the Older Ones.

And that's when Jodi said, "This is probably the worst day of my life."

And Zach said he thought it was going to be cool. But that's only because all the girls in 6B think he's great, and one time when they came to our class to help us with our maths, Zach kept getting all the answers wrong, and all the girls in 6B kept saying, "Aww. He's so cute."

But then every time I asked **MY** one for help, she just shrugged and flicked to the

back where the answers are, which we are **NEVER** allowed to do. And she never called me cute once, or even said **ONE WORD** to me.

So anyway, once the assembly was over, we all went to 6B's classroom. Miss Jones was already there, and she'd brought down all of our workbooks and stuff from our classroom and none of it was wet, which I thought was weird because of leaks in the roof.

Then we saw that Miss Jones had put up a big curtain in the middle of the classroom so we couldn't see into 6B's bit, and so they couldn't see into our bit. Then Miss

Jones told us all to go and find a new seat. So me, and Maisie, and Jodi, and Zach all managed to squeeze around just one table, next to the curtain, and it was better than being in our own classroom actually, because in our own classroom we don't get to sit at the same table any more, because of

sometimes being a **"BAD INFLUENCE"** on each other. But Miss Jones didn't say anything about that in the new classroom.

But then during the lesson, things kept getting thrown over the curtain from 6B's side. And then somebody poked me in the back through the curtain, so I shouted, **"HEY!"** And then someone behind the curtain burst out laughing, and Miss Jones sighed and told us to move our table forward as much as we could, so we did.

Then when we were doing our maths, we could hear 6B doing their maths too because the curtain wasn't soundproof, and Jodi kept saying about how their maths sounded easy, and that she should probably be doing it. So I was just about to ask Jodi to multiply 139 by 87 in her head, since she thought she was so brainy at maths, but then I heard someone on the other side of the curtain whispering about the REAL reason loads of the school was

"OUT OF BOUNDS".

So I said, "Shhhh! Listen!" and Jodi stopped talking and we all listened. But we

couldn't hear properly because we were too far away. So every time Miss Jones wasn't looking, we moved our table a bit closer to the curtain again, until we were even closer than we'd been when the curtain finger poked me.

And that's when we heard one of the 6B's saying that there WEREN'T any leaks in the roof, and that it hadn't even been raining last night, and that the REAL reason for the "OUT OF BOUNDS" was because the school had RATS!

And that's when Maisie fainted and pulled
the whole curtain down with her.

Rat
Bag

On Tuesday it was horrible walking to school because it was raining really hard, and the sky was really dark like it was still night time, and also because I was freaked out about all the RATS at our school.

Then when we met Jodi and Maisie outside

the classroom, I got a bit of a fright because Maisie had big dark circles under her eyes, and she was wearing plastic bags over her shoes, and she wasn't really blinking.

Jodi said that she'd had to tie the bags on Maisie's feet just to get her to come inside, because Maisie was scared that the rats were going to get in her shoes. I didn't think that that really made any sense, but I didn't say anything because Maisie looked in a bit of a state.

Then Zach made a face and said, "What's that smell?"

And Maisie said, "It's a dead rat." And then she pointed to her bag.

Then Maisie started whisper-shouting, which is when you try to whisper something but you end up kind of shouting it, even though you're still whispering.

And she said, "It must've sneaked into my bag at lunch time, and I've not been able to open it, and I've not been able to do my homework, and I heard it eating my pencils

all night, and I couldn't sleep, but then it went quiet, and I think it died, and—"

But then before Maisie could even finish what she was saying Jodi opened Maisie's bag and emptied it on to the ground. And there weren't any dead rats inside, just a leftover tuna sandwich that was stinking.

So Maisie started doing her homework really quickly, and Jodi put the sandwich in the bin. But then the bell went and Miss Jones opened the classroom door and said that everyone had to line up outside because we were going to ANOTHER assembly!

I thought for SURE that this one was going to be about the rats, and the whole way down to the assembly hall I was getting a bit worried because Zach kept saying things about how the rats had probably killed someone and that was why they had to tell us the truth about the rats, so that we could protect ourselves, because rats carry diseases, like measles and chicken pox and the Plague, and all the stuff he was saying was making me want to have plastic bags tied over my shoes too.

When we got to the assembly hall, everyone sat on the ground except for us and 6B, who just crouched down a little bit and pretended to sit, because we all knew about the rats.

Then everyone went really quiet and all you could hear was the rain hitting off the big window, and I didn't know why everyone had gone so quiet all of a sudden until I looked at the stage and saw that there was a really tall, scary-looking man just standing there STARING at us.

Zach said, "Who's that?" And I said that I didn't know.

And Jodi said, "He looks weird." And we all nodded. Then Maisie grabbed my hand and dug her nails in.

And that's when the man said, "Good morning. I'm your new Head Teacher."

And then there was a really loud clap of thunder outside. And everyone started screaming.

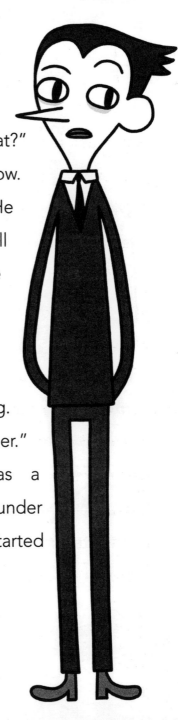

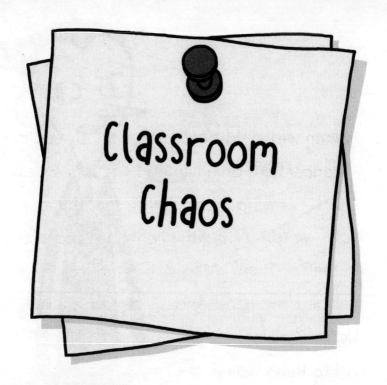

Classroom Chaos

The assembly had to be cancelled because of all the screaming, and because most of 1B were crying, and because one of them must have had an "accident" because the caretaker had to come with his mop and bucket.

When we got back to class, nobody could concentrate on anything Miss Jones was saying because of the thunder, and the lightning, and also because of the scary new Head Teacher.

Miss Jones had to keep telling us to settle down, and to stop screaming every time the thunder went, or the lightning flashed, but we couldn't, and Jodi kept saying over and over again about how weird all of this was, and she was right. I mean, we already HAD a Head Teacher;

Mr Murphy was our Head Teacher. It didn't make any sense.

Then Zach whispered, "Where's Mr Murphy gone?" So I said that I was going to ask Miss Jones what was going on right away, because Miss Jones would definitely know because she is actually getting MARRIED to Mr Murphy (which is a bit disgusting) and last term he gave her an engagement ring and everything.

So Jodi said that she would come up to the front with me, but before we could even stand up, Gary Petrie put his hand up and said, "Miss, where's Mr Murphy?"

Everyone went silent and stared at Miss Jones to see what she would say. But then Miss Jones's face went a bit weird, and she said, "We have a new Head Teacher now, and that is that." And she said it with a bit of a shaky voice, so none of us asked any more questions because we could all see that Miss Jones looked weird in the face.

Then Zach said, "Something's wrong. Miss Jones looks upset." And we all knew that he was right.

Then Jodi said, "I don't like this new Head Teacher one bit. I mean, where did he even come from? And where IS Mr Murphy?"

And I was just thinking about how weird everything was getting because of having to move classroom, and all the rats, and the new scary Head Teacher and Mr Murphy disappearing, when there was a loud knock on the classroom door and Maisie did a yelpy noise.

We all went really quiet because we were

SURE it was going to be the new Head Teacher. But it wasn't. It was one of the office ladies. And she had a note.

We all watched while Miss Jones read it. Then she asked us to all sit up straight and listen very closely, so we did. And I looked at Maisie and saw that her face had gone a bit blue so I nudged her and she started breathing again, because sometimes you have to do that when Maisie gets scared and forgets to breathe.

And then Jodi whispered, "I really don't want to go to another assembly." And I DEFINITELY didn't want to go to one either. But it wasn't another assembly. It was worse.

Miss Jones said that the new Head Teacher

wanted to see us all in his office! And that we had to go in twos, and that he wanted to meet us and get to know us all!

And then Miss Jones said, "Izzy and Zach, you can go first. Off you go."

As soon as we got to the new Head Teacher's office, Zach got scared and said, "I'm not going in."

And I said, "What?"

And he said, "He's too scary. I'm not going. You go."

Then Zach tried to go back up the stairs, but I caught him by his sleeve and said, "I'm

not going in on my OWN!"

And then Zach said that we should just both go back up to the classroom and pretend that we'd been. And that sounded like a good idea, so I said, "OK, what will we say if Miss Jones asks us about what the new Head Teacher said to us?"

And Zach didn't say anything, because Zach is TERRIBLE at making up lies on the spot, and one time when he got caught copying my homework he said that he was just making a copy for me so I could put it up in a frame, and then he started crying.

So anyway, I said that when we got back

to the classroom, we should just go right up to Miss Jones and say that the new Head Teacher had asked us what our favourite colour was, and that I had said orange and that Zach had said green. And that we had asked him what his favourite colour was, and that he had said blue, and that it had been nice to get to know us.

But then Zach said that that was too much to remember, and also that he didn't want to say that green was his favourite colour, because it wasn't any more, and because blue was his favourite colour now. But then I said that it didn't really matter that green wasn't his REAL favourite colour because it was just part of the plan, and also that he couldn't say that blue was his favourite colour because that was what we were going to say the new Head Teacher's favourite colour was. And that if they were the same then that might sound too

SUSPICIOUS

and then Miss Jones might not believe us.

I was starting to get really annoyed with Zach because he ALWAYS has to make easy stuff more complicated, when we both noticed that the new Head Teacher was standing RIGHT THERE and that he'd probably heard EVERYTHING we'd just said, because we hadn't even heard his door opening and so he could have been there the whole time!

I looked up at him, and he looked even taller and scarier than he had at the assembly. He had weird big black eyes, and he wasn't smiling or anything.

Then he said, "Do come in."

And Zach just looked at me with his mouth hanging wide open.

And we couldn't really do anything except go in. So we did.

Get Us Out Of Here!!!

It was really dark inside the new Head Teacher's office. Much darker than when it was Mr Murphy's office, and it looked different too.

There was a huge fancy desk that hadn't been there before, and it looked really old like an antique or something, and there were all these weird ornaments, and a statue thing of just someone's head and a bit of their shoulders, but with no body. And all the curtains were shut, and it smelled funny, and there was a big empty box folded up

by the door that said **"FRAGILE. HANDLE WITH CARE."** And I wondered what had been in it.

We watched as the new Head Teacher sat down at the big desk. Then he pointed to two chairs and said, "Please."

I wasn't a hundred per cent sure what he wanted us to do with the chairs, and I thought that maybe he wanted us to bring them to him, but then Zach sat down, so I sat down too.

Then the new Head Teacher said, "I would very much like to get to know all of my pupils. Please, tell me something interesting about yourselves. Do you have any hobbies? How about flying? I love to fly. But sometimes my arms get a little tired."

And then he laughed a bit, but it sounded weird. And then he just stared at us.

I had **NO IDEA** what to say, and all I could think about was how **SCARY** his eyes were, and how pale his face was, and how his lips looked like two little red worms.

And then I saw it: the photograph on the wall behind him. And I think

I must have jumped in my seat a bit, but I don't think the new Head Teacher noticed because he was too busy listening to Zach who had started going on and on about how his favourite colour used to be green, but that now it was blue, but that he still wasn't a hundred per cent sure. I couldn't take my eyes off the photo, and even though I wasn't sure what it meant, I knew that it wasn't good.

And then the new Head Teacher said, "And what about you, Isabella?"

And I do not like it when people who are not my mum, or dad, or gran call me that. And I don't even really like it when THEY

call me that. But I especially didn't like it when the new Head Teacher said it. So even though I was scared of him, I said, "My name is Izzy, actually."

And that made the new Head Teacher's eyes go a bit wide. And his worm lips curled up a bit at the side. And then he said, "How interesting." Even though it wasn't.

Then all of a sudden Zach said, "Are you going to a funeral today?"

And I couldn't BELIEVE Zach had said that! Or why he was even asking any questions at all!

And the new Head Teacher said, "I am not.

Why do you ask, Zachary?"

And Zach said, "Oh. Um. I don't know."

But I knew that Zach DID know exactly why he'd asked him that. And that it was because the new Head Teacher was dressed like he was going to a funeral and even his tie was black.

Then the new Head Teacher said, "Ah. Is it because my name is Mr Graves?"

And I almost fell off my seat, and Zach gasped, because this was probably the CREEPIEST name we had ever heard!

I just stared at Zach and begged him with my eyes not to ask any more questions

because I just wanted to get

OUT OF THERE.

Then Zach went quiet, and started biting his nails.

And then the new Head Teacher said, "I shall let you both get back to class now. Good day."

And then Zach said, "Good night," because he was totally freaked out. And I got up right away, and pulled Zach by the arm so we could get out quicker.

But then Zach saw it. And he froze.

And the new Head Teacher must've noticed us both staring at the photo behind him on the wall, because he turned to see what it was we were looking at.

And then he said, "Ah, yes. That is a very old photograph. It was taken when—"

But we didn't even wait to hear the rest, we just ran out the door before he could turn around.

The Cape

When we got outside we almost ran right into Jodi and Maisie.

And Jodi said, "We're next. What's it like?"

I looked at Zach, and Zach looked at me, and then he started biting his nails again.

I knew that there wasn't enough time to

tell them about everything, and I looked at Maisie and saw that her eyes were starting to do that thing where she goes a bit cross-eyed before she faints, so I said, "Just come back to the classroom with us. OK?"

And I said it in a certain way that I knew Jodi would understand. And Jodi looked at me in the way that I knew she got it. And that she knew something had gone SERIOUSLY wrong, and that there was

NO WAY

they should go into the new Head Teacher's office.

But then the new Head Teacher appeared.

And he said, "Jodi. Maisie-Ann-Margaret. Do come in."

And we all knew it was too late. So Maisie

went in, and Jodi started to follow her. But before Jodi could even get all the way in we heard a thump. And we knew that it was Maisie fainting. And that she must have seen the photograph too.

Once the ambulance had gone, me and Zach and Jodi were made to go back to class.

When we got back Miss Jones asked what had taken us so long and where Maisie was. So I explained about how Maisie had fainted, and that the new Head Teacher had called an ambulance, and about how one of the office ladies had phoned Maisie's mum, and about how Maisie's mum had come running into the school screaming,

WHERE IS SHE?!"

and about how Maisie's mum had to lie down on a stretcher and wear an oxygen mask because she started breathing weird, and about how they all went away to the hospital in the ambulance even though Maisie was awake again, and back to normal.

And Miss Jones just said, "OK." Because Miss Jones knows that Maisie faints all the time, and that there isn't really anything you can do about it, and that it was probably just because the new Head Teacher wasn't used to it that he must have got a fright and phoned the ambulance instead of just waiting for her to wake up, like we do.

So we went and sat down and Jodi said, "Say nothing." And then she pointed to

the curtain. And we nodded. And then she whispered, "The Den." And we nodded again.

As soon as it was break time we ran to The Den.

The Den is our secret place under the stairs that go up to the toilets. It used to be the old caretaker's store cupboard, but then he left. And we used to have the only key, but then we lost it. But it's OK because nobody knows about The Den except for us (and Mathilde, but she lives in France) so it's perfect for having important meetings when you don't want nosy people, like 6B, hearing all your secrets.

But when we got to The Den, we couldn't believe it! There was a big banner right across the stairs and past The Den, which said, "DANGER. NO ENTRY."

And Zach said,

"THE RATS!"

And I said, "Oh!" because I'd actually completely forgotten about all the rats because of scary Mr Graves.

But then Jodi said, "Stay here." And she ducked right under the barrier and went in anyway.

After about two minutes she came back out, and her knees were dirty, like she'd been crawling about the floor, and she had a mop in her hand.

And she said, "All clear. Come on." So we went in. And I expected to see rat blood everywhere, because Jodi was looking a bit mad, and I thought she might have squished some of the rats with the mop. But then she said that she'd done a COMPLETE SWEEP, and that there wasn't a single rat in The Den, and that as long as we remembered to shut the door when we left, The Den should remain a

SECURE ZONE.

So we all sat down on our buckets, and Zach went to fill up the kettle in the little

sink and make us all cups of tea, but then Jodi said, "No tea. Tell me what happened in there!"

So Zach sat back down. And we told Jodi all about how the new Head Teacher's office was weird, and dark, and about how it smelled funny. And then we told her about the old desk, and the weird statues. And I told her all about the big folded-up box by the door that had said

"FRAGILE. HANDLE WITH CARE."

And then we told Jodi about how the new Head Teacher's name was actually Mr Graves, and her eyes went wide.

And then I looked at Zach. And Zach looked at Jodi. And then Zach said, "Mr Graves has a photo up on the wall behind his desk."

And then he took a deep breath and said, "It's a picture of him wearing a long black

And Jodi said, "A cape? Why would he be wearing a cape? Only Batman wears a cape.

Or vampires." And then she gasped and covered her mouth with her hands.

And I said, **"EXACTLY!"**

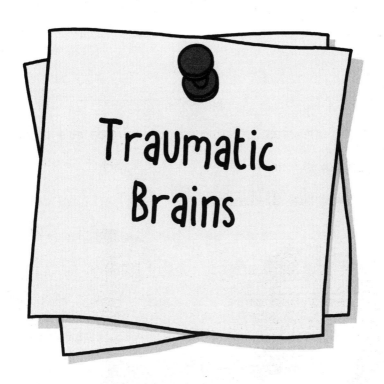

Traumatic
Brains

That night Jodi said that we all had to attend a secret meeting at her house after our tea. And she even got her mum to phone Maisie's mum to see if Maisie could come too, but Maisie's mum said no. And she said it was because Maisie had fainted again when the new Head Teacher had phoned to see how she was.

And we all knew that Maisie had probably fainted because she had probably been the one who answered the phone. And Mr Graves had probably said, "Hello, this is your Head Teacher, Mr Graves, speaking." And Maisie wouldn't have known about his name being Mr Graves, and she would have got a big shock.

So anyway, when me and Zach got to Jodi's house, we all went into Jodi's room and Jodi put up the **"SECRET MEETING"** sign on her bedroom door so that Jodi's mum knew

that we were having a meeting, so not to disturb us, and also to bring snacks.

Then Jodi said, "The secret meeting has officially begun."

And I said that it was Zach's turn to do the notes, and I gave him a FIRM look because Zach NEVER does the notes and he always tries to get out of it by saying that his hand is hurting.

And then Jodi said, "I'll start." And then she said, "I'm not sure about Mr Graves being a vampire."

And then Zach said, "But what about the cape?"

And Jodi said, "It might have just been a Batman cape."

And I was a hundred per cent sure it hadn't been a batman cape, so I said, "Jodi. It definitely wasn't a Batman cape. It was a creepy, scary, vampire cape, like from Olden Times."

And Zach nodded loads.

But then Jodi said, "Well, maybe it was a

vampire cape then, but maybe Mr Graves was just dressed up as a vampire for Halloween."

And I didn't say anything, because I thought that Jodi was maybe right, because last year Zach dressed up as a vampire on Halloween, and I have a photo of him at home with tomato soup all over his face, because we didn't have any ketchup

at my house to use for the blood, because Dad had forgot to put it on **THE LIST** when he finished it all, and Mum fell out with him about it.

But then Zach told Jodi about how when Mr Graves had caught us looking at it, that he had said that it was a **VERY OLD** photo, even though he didn't look any younger in the photo, and that he just looked the same. And how that was proof that Mr Graves was a vampire, because vampires are **VERY OLD** but they don't age like people, and that they always stay looking young.

But then Jodi said that she **STILL** didn't

think just one photo was enough proof to be sure FOR A FACT that Mr Graves was a vampire, even if he was really creepy.

So that's when I explained to Jodi about how DARK it had been in Mr Graves's office. And about how PALE his skin had looked. And about how red his weird worm lips were, and that they were probably all wormy and red because of drinking loads of blood.

Jodi said that she agreed that his office being so dark and having all the blinds shut was GOOD EVIDENCE that the new Head Teacher was maybe a vampire, because she said she knew that vampires HATED the

sunlight, because it made them
BURN.

But then she said that she still wasn't
sure about the photo, and that the new
Head Teacher's lips were probably just red
because he'd been drinking Ribena.

But then Zach said, "But it wasn't just him
in the photo!"

And I didn't really know what Zach meant,
because I didn't remember seeing anything
else in the photo. But then all

of a sudden I remembered.

And I COULDN'T BELIEVE that I'd forgotten all about it!

And that's when I shouted, "It wasn't just Mr Graves in the photo! There were MORE!"

And I stood up, because this was serious, and I couldn't believe what I'd just remembered.

And Jodi said, "More what?"

And I said, "VAMPIRES, Jodi! There were LOADS OF THEM!"

Lies, Blood and Strawberry Milkshake

After I remembered about all the other vampires in the photo, we explained to Jodi about how there had been loads of other people standing in the distance, behind Mr Graves, and that they had all been wearing long capes too. And then Zach said that Mr

Graves must be the head of some sort of vampire army.

And then Jodi held my hand and started patting it. And she said that I must have forgotten all about the other vampires in the photo because it was too TRAUMATIC for my brain to remember. And then she told us all about how she'd read a story in one of her mum's magazines about this man, and how he forgot all about being involved in a SHARK ATTACK because it had been a TRAUMATIC EXPERIENCE and was too scary for his brain to remember. And that twenty years later the man remembered

everything all of a sudden when he went into a supermarket and saw a can of tuna.

Then Jodi said that she thought we were right about Mr Graves, but that we needed to be a hundred per cent sure if we were going to do something about it, like go to the police or phone the government. Jodi said we needed to come up with a plan to get more evidence. And she was right.

So I said that we should start by telling each other EVERYTHING that we already knew about vampires and then write a list. So we did. And this is what we wrote:

VAMPIRES

1. They drink blood

2. They are very pale (because they are dead, even though they look like they are alive)

3. They are very old (but still look young)

4. They wear long black capes

5. They have fangs for biting people

6. They hate the sunlight because it makes them burn and turn to dust

And then Jodi said that we needed to find out more, and that we could use her mum's computer to do the research.

So Zach looked up **"VAMPIRES"** because he's the best on computers, and that's when he found an old black-and-white picture of a vampire, and I **SWEAR** it looked **EXACTLY** like Mr Graves, and I was almost ninety-eight per cent sure it was him.

Then Zach started reading out the stuff that was written underneath the photo and that's when we found out **LOADS** more stuff about vampires, like how they sleep in **COFFINS**, and that they can do

MIND CONTROL,

and also that they are REPELLED by garlic.

And then I got a bit worried that I might have a tiny bit of vampireness inside me, like from my great-great-uncle or something, because I am DEFINITELY repelled by garlic, and I won't even eat my lasagne if Mum lets the garlic bread touch it.

But then Zach said that he hated garlic too, and that it was stinking, and that loads of people hate it, and that there was a difference between hating to eat it and being REPELLED by it.

So I took the list and I added:

7.   They are repelled by garlic

8.   They sleep in a coffin

9.   They can do mind control

Then Zach said that he'd found something else, and that it was a clip from an old film about vampires. And I knew that it was a **REALLY** old film because it was in black and white.

So we all started watching it, and the music was really creepy, and then the coffin made this really loud creaking sound, and the vampire woke up and sat up in the coffin, and then he showed his fangs and started **HISSING** at this woman, and then she started screaming, and the music went all dramatic, and then the vampire jumped on the woman and bit her right in the neck!

And that's when Jodi's mum came rushing in and said that we shouldn't be using the computer without asking her first, and that we were too young for vampire films, and also that the film was silly and not what real vampires are like at all.

So that's when I said, "What ARE real vampires like?"

And Jodi's mum sat down for ages and started telling us all about how vampires

are very beautiful, and about how they are very romantic, and then she went on and on about this one called Edward for ages.

I was a bit surprised about vampires being beautiful, because I didn't think Mr Graves was very beautiful, and I didn't really think that boys could be beautiful.

Then Zach asked Jodi's mum how she knew so much about vampires. And that's when Jodi's mum said that she'd read all these really famous vampire books, and that they were all about vampires, and also that she'd even seen all the films. So she obviously knew what she was talking about.

And then Jodi said, "How can vampires be nice if they bite people and drink their blood?"

And Jodi's mum thought for a bit, but then she asked us if we wanted strawberry milkshake, and even though she hadn't answered our question, we all said yes because Jodi's mum makes THE BEST strawberry milkshake in the world, and it's so pink that it even glows in the dark a bit. And there's still a pink stain on Jodi's carpet that you can see when the lights are off, from when Maisie had five glasses and was pink-sick on it.

Then when Jodi's mum went to get the milkshakes, Jodi said that she thought her mum was LYING to us. And that she didn't believe vampires were any of the things that her mum had told us. And that her mum was making it all up because she didn't want us to know the TRUTH about vampires because she probably just thought we were too young to know, and that it would scare us.

And then Jodi said that she knew FOR A FACT that her mum had been lying to us, because when we had asked her about the human blood, she didn't even answer the question, and that she had just CHANGED THE SUBJECT.

Then Jodi said that that's what grown-ups ALWAYS do when they don't want to tell you something, or they don't want to tell you the truth.

And I thought that Jodi was DEFINITELY right, because my mum does that too! Like the time Gran bought Mum a very special jumper for Christmas, and it was bright green with a bit of fur on it and it even had little bells on the shoulders that jingled when Mum

moved. Mum told Gran that she loved it, and she even put it on right away and wore it all Christmas Day. But then a few weeks later when me and Mum were taking old clothes to the charity shop, I heard something inside one of the bags JINGLING and when I asked Mum about it she went a bit weird and started asking me all about my homework, and about my washing basket. That's when I knew that she was just trying to CHANGE THE SUBJECT because she didn't want to tell me the truth, which was that she had told a LIE to Gran about loving the jumper and that she had put it in the charity bag!

So that's when Jodi said that we shouldn't add any of the things her mum had said to the list since it was

HIGHLY UNRELIABLE INFORMATION.

And that we should only add the stuff from the film. So I added **HISSING** because the vampire had made this really weird hissing sound before he bit the lady in the neck.

Then Jodi said that she would try to read all the vampire books and watch all the films tonight when her mum was sleeping, and we said OK.

So when Jodi's mum came back in with the milkshake, we said that we weren't doing the meeting on vampires any more, and that we were doing it on grass. And that we didn't need her to stay and tell us anything about grass because we knew it all. But I don't

think she believed us, because she looked at us for ages, and then she unplugged the laptop and took it with her when she left.

And then Zach's mobile phone beeped. And it was a text. And it was from Maisie, which was weird because I didn't even know that Maisie had a mobile phone, because I'd never seen it before, and I thought that Zach was the only one who had one.

And then Zach read the text out loud. And this is what it said:

THE NEW HEAD TEACHER PHONED MY HOUSE. HIS NAME IS MR GRAVES. WE HAVE TO MOVE SCHOOLS.

So we told Maisie we thought Mr Graves might be a vampire. But Maisie didn't text back. And we knew it was because the text must have been too much for her. And that we probably shouldn't have sent it.

Rat
Poo
Shoe

On Wednesday, Maisie was back at school. And as soon as me and Zach met her outside our new classroom, we told her all the stuff we'd found out at the secret meeting, about the garlic, and the coffins, and the hissing, and the mind-control.

And then Maisie had to lie down on the ground outside the classroom, so me and Zach just lay down with her because it had been a very hard week for us all.

But then we remembered about the rats and we all jumped up at the same time. And then Maisie started crying because she said there was a rat poo on the ground, and that it had definitely touched her when she had been lying down.

I thought that it was probably just a raisin, but I wasn't a hundred per cent sure, so I decided to be brave and squish it a bit with my shoe. And it WAS a raisin, so Maisie

stopped crying.

When the bell went for class, I thought it was weird that Jodi wasn't there yet, but we went in and sat down anyway. Miss Jones must have thought it was weird that Jodi wasn't there either because she said, "Where's Jodi this morning?" But I just said that we didn't know. And then Miss Jones asked to speak to Maisie at her desk, and I knew it was to see if she was OK after having to go away in the ambulance yesterday.

And then when Miss Jones was busy speaking to Maisie, Jodi came in. And she looked really weird, and her hair didn't look like it usually did, because it usually didn't have bits sticking up all over the place.

Then Jodi said, "I tried to read all the vampire books when my mum went to sleep last night, but they were really boring, and I kept falling asleep."

And I felt a bit bad because I'd just had a piece of toast and gone right to bed when I got home, and I hadn't done any research at all.

Then Jodi said, "So I got my mum to drop me off early this morning, and I went on the computers in the library before the bell. And I found **THIS**."

And that's when we looked at the bit of paper Jodi had printed out.

And at the top it said:

VAMPIRE BATS

And that's when Jodi told us that she'd found out all about vampire bats, and about

how vampires can change themselves into bats, and then change back into vampires. And about how they change into bats so they can sneak up on people and bite them. And about how they can change back into a bat really quickly and fly away when people are trying to catch them.

And then Zach looked at me and said, "That's why we didn't hear him coming out of his office! He must've flown out as a bat, and then changed!"

But I didn't really believe it, because I'd never heard anything about people turning into animals before.

So I said, "Jodi, do you really think that the new Head Teacher is a vampire bat?"

And then Jodi looked very serious. And she looked over both her shoulders to make sure nobody was listening. And then she said, "No, actually. I think the new Head Teacher is a

Give Us Garlic Bread

When Miss Jones was doing the register, Jodi told us that even though she couldn't find anything on the internet in the library about vampires being able to turn into rats, that didn't mean they couldn't. And that the only reason she probably couldn't find out about it was because the computers in the school library stop you from being able to look at most websites.

Then Jodi said that the word RAT was almost the same as the word BAT. And also that rats are just like bats, but without wings. But I still didn't believe it.

But then Jodi said, "Think about it! All of a sudden there are RATS in the school. And then all of a sudden there is a NEW Head Teacher who is probably definitely a vampire! These two things are DEFINITELY NOT A COINCIDENCE!"

So I thought about it. And that's when I

realised that it made sense.

So I said, "Well, if vampires can turn into rats, and Mr Graves is a vampire rat, then we've got an even BIGGER problem than we thought!"

And Jodi said, "What do you mean?"

And I said, "Well, what about all the other rats? There are probably HUNDREDS of them in the school!"

And then Zach whispered, "The Army."

And for a minute I thought Zach meant that we were going to have to get the real army in, which sounded like a good idea. But I knew that Jodi would just say that we

couldn't phone them until we had enough EVIDENCE, because she is OBSESSED with evidence. But then the whole table started shaking, and I noticed that Maisie was back.

And then Maisie said, "Vampire Rat Army."

And Zach nodded.

And I knew that we needed to come up with the best plan we had EVER come up with, or the school was going to be taken over by an army of vampire rats!

That afternoon, we all said that we'd eat our lunch as quick as we could, and then go to The Den to make a plan. But then at

lunchtime, something happened.

When we got to the dinner hall, we saw that it was THEMED DINNERS today. And I just KNEW that there was going to be GARLIC BREAD because every time the dinner ladies do THEMED DINNERS, it's ALWAYS Italian Day, even though me and Zach always put LOADS of suggestions in the SUGGESTION BOX, like JUNGLE DAY and APOCALYPSE DAY.

So anyway, I knew that there was going to be garlic bread, because when it's Italian Day we always get lasagne, spaghetti bolognaise, pizza, and GARLIC BREAD.

So Jodi said that we should all eat as much garlic bread as we could, so that Mr Graves and all the vampire rats would be REPELLED by us because we smelled of garlic. And even though me and Zach both HATE garlic bread, we said OK, because we needed to do it to protect our lives.

But then when we went up to the counter and Jodi asked if she could have some garlic bread, the dinner lady said that there wasn't any! And we all looked at each other because that was very SUSPICIOUS.

Then when we sat down, Jodi said that she couldn't concentrate, and that she wasn't

even hungry any more, even though pizza is one of her favourites. She said that we just HAD to find out why there wasn't any garlic bread when it was Italian Day, and that we needed to find out if it had anything to do with Mr Graves. And we all agreed, because if Mr Graves HAD told the dinner ladies not to make it, then that would be evidence that he was a vampire.

So Zach said that we should just go up and ask the dinner ladies about it. But then Maisie said that we couldn't because Mrs Kidd (the evil dinner monitor) would tell us off for being out of our seats.

But then Jodi said that she didn't care, and she got up anyway. So I went with her, for support, because the dinner ladies don't really like Jodi after the time she was a vegetarian and she accused one of the dinner ladies of hiding a sausage under her mash

ON PURPOSE

so that she would eat it by mistake, and not be a vegetarian any more. And Jodi got so upset she had a JT (which means a Jodi Tantrum) and then she got a detention. And

I got one too, because Mrs Kidd said that I had been ENCOURAGING Jodi, even though I didn't even say

ONE WORD!

So anyway, we went up to the counter, and Jodi said, "Excuse me, please." But we couldn't get any of the dinner ladies' attention, because they were standing in the back, and because everyone had already been served, and also because they don't like us.

So we started sniffing all the empty trays, because I said maybe there **HAD** been garlic bread, but that because we were last to go up for dinners that day, maybe it had just run out by the time we got there.

But then one of the dinner ladies came rushing out and told us to take our noses out of her trays **"RIGHT NOW"**. And then she said, "Oh. It's **YOU**." And she said it in a really horrible way. And she looked **RIGHT** at Jodi when she said it.

And I was a bit worried that Jodi was maybe going to give her cheek, and that we'd both get into trouble again, and also that we wouldn't get to ask her about the garlic bread. But then I heard a dog barking. And I knew right away that it wasn't a real dog, and that it was Zach. And that he was doing it as a **SIGNAL** to us to say that Mrs

Kidd was on her way over.

So I said, "Jodi, hurry! Just ask her! Ask her!"

And Jodi said, "Why isn't there any garlic bread?" And then she said, "Please," because the dinner lady still looked cross at us for sniffing her trays.

The dinner lady started pulling all the trays out, and banging them all over the place, and I thought she was just going to completely ignore our question.

But then she said, "Banned."

And we said, "What?"

And that made the dinner lady groan a

bit. And then she said, "BANNED! The new Head Teacher banned it!"

And even though I was already ninety-nine per cent sure that Mr Graves was a vampire, I was still completely SHOCKED. And even though Mrs Kidd told us off for being out of our seats, and sent us to sit in the TIME OUT chairs outside the office for fifteen minutes, we didn't care, because now we had GARLIC EVIDENCE.

When we were sitting in the TIME OUT chairs, we heard the office ladies gossiping about Mr Graves. So we listened very closely, and that's when we heard one of them say, "He's not really strict, he's just nervous. It's sweet, really." And then another one said, "He's so young. Bless his cotton socks." And then they all giggled.

I couldn't BELIEVE what I was hearing, because Mr Graves DEFINITELY wasn't young OR sweet! He looked like he was at least thirty, and he was the SCARIEST person EVER!

But then Jodi looked at me and whispered, "MIND CONTROL!" And I nodded, because I knew that she must be right, and that Mr Graves must have mind-controlled the office ladies into thinking he was young and sweet and innocent so that they wouldn't find out he was a blood-sucking vampire!

But then we heard WHISPERING coming from inside the Head Teacher's office, and it sounded very SUSPICIOUS.

So we looked to see if the office ladies were watching us, but they weren't. So we tip-toed up to the Head Teacher's office, held our breath and put our ears up against the door.

And that's when we heard Mr Graves say, "Hello, my darling. What a beautiful lady you are." And then he started HISSING!

The Biggest Pencil in the World

As soon as the office lady told us our fifteen minutes were up, we RAN to The Den to tell Zach and Maisie about the hissing. But when we got there, Zach and Maisie weren't even inside The Den yet, they were just standing at the door. And then Zach said that it was

because of Maisie and the **"DANGER. NO ENTRY"** sign.

So we explained to Maisie about how Jodi had made sure that The Den was a **SECURE ZONE** and that as long as we kept the door shut, no rats would be able to get in. So Maisie said OK, and that she'd go in, but that she wanted to put her plastic bags back on her feet first. So Jodi helped her put them on.

And then when we were going in, I was first, and I noticed that the door actually **WASN'T** shut all the way, and that there was a tiny little gap, but I didn't say anything, because I

didn't want Maisie to faint, and also because I thought that the gap was way too small for a big fat vampire rat to get through anyway.

Once we were all inside, and the secret meeting had officially begun, we told Zach and Maisie about what the dinner lady had said about garlic bread being BANNED and also about the HISSING!

That's when Maisie said that we should all DEFINITELY bring garlic sandwiches to school tomorrow, to protect ourselves, and everyone agreed. Because we knew that Mr Graves had probably bitten that beautiful lady in his office, and drunk her blood, like

that vampire in the old film did.

Then Jodi said that we were going to have to do something before things got even more

OUT OF CONTROL.

And we all agreed except for Maisie, who said that we should just hide in The Den until it was time to go to secondary school.

And that's when Zach started to tell us that he knew about ways to kill vampires. And that you needed to put a steak through their heart. And I said that that didn't make any sense. But then Zach said that he didn't mean a steak you eat, and that he meant a **WOODEN STAKE**, that was shaped like a big, sharp pencil.

And then Jodi said she actually had one of those, and that her gran had got her one from Benidorm last year. And that it had a giant rubber on the end of it, and pictures of the beach all over it. And Zach said that Jodi should **DEFINITELY** bring it with her

to school tomorrow.

But Maisie said that she **DEFINITELY** shouldn't. And that we should just do something to scare the new Head Teacher away, so that he went to another school and left us alone and didn't drink our blood.

And that's when Jodi jumped up and shouted, "Garlic muffins!"

And I said that I would **MAYBE** eat a garlic sandwich if I was allowed to put crisps, or ketchup, or something else on it too, but there was **NO WAY** I was going to eat a garlic muffin.

But Jodi just smiled. And then she said, "It's not for you."

When we got back to class, Jodi said that she was going to ask her mum if they could bake chocolate muffins tonight, and that she would get her mum to let her make one garlic muffin too, and that we would give it to Mr Graves.

Zach said he thought it was a brilliant idea. And that if Mr Graves was REPELLED by the smell of garlic, then eating it would probably make him turn into a rat as soon as he ate it and run far away, as far away as Australia, and that all his vampire rat army would go with him because he was the leader.

I agreed that it was a brilliant idea, and I also said that I thought Jodi should make two garlic muffins, just in case one got burnt in the oven or something.

And then Maisie asked if Jodi could please make three because she likes garlic and thought they sounded lovely, and so Jodi said OK.

But then we heard Miss Ross through the classroom curtain telling 6B that the new Head Teacher was on his way up to the classroom! And all of a sudden Maisie's body went really weird. And she went really straight, like a stick. And her eyes went even wider than I thought human eyes could go before your eyeballs fall out! And then she started making this weird low sound that I've never heard her do before, and it kind of sounded like when my cats start fighting each other. And then she went

completely silent.

So I said, "Maisie, are you OK?" But she didn't reply. And she was doing that weird staring thing that people do, when your eyes go wide, and you stare, but you don't really stare AT anything. So I waved my hand in front of her face, but she didn't blink. And then Jodi waved her hand in front of Maisie's face too. Nothing.

And that's when I realised that hearing about Mr Graves coming up to our classroom must have been TOO MUCH for Maisie. And that Maisie's brain was TRAUMATISED.

And then Zach said, "What do we do?"

And Jodi said that maybe we should get
Miss Jones. But I said no, and that we should
try to fix Maisie's brain ourselves, because I
had an idea.

So I flicked to the back of my notebook,
and I wrote something in big letters, and
then I held it up to Maisie's face. And it said,

MAISIE. ARE YOU IN THERE?
BLINK ONCE FOR YES
AND TWICE FOR NO.

And we all waited to see what Maisie
would do. And then she blinked once. So

we knew that she was still with us. But then she started lifting her hand up into the air REALLY slowly, and we all got really freaked out because we didn't know what she was doing.

And then Zach said, "Oh NO! Vampire mind control!"

And we all STARED at Maisie, and moved our seats away from her a bit.

And then Maisie's arm went even higher into the air. And then it went really straight, and her finger started to point slowly.

And then Zach said, "Mr Graves is making her do that!"

Then I realised what Maisie was doing. So I said, "Look! She's pointing at something." So we looked at where we thought Maisie was pointing, but all we could see was the bookshelf.

And then Jodi said, "Maisie, are you having your mind controlled right now?"

And Maisie blinked twice, for no.

But then Zach said that Maisie might not be telling the truth if she was under the mind control of a vampire.

So then I said, "Maisie, are you just pointing at something?"

And Maisie blinked once.

So we looked again to see if we could see what she was pointing at. And that's when Zach screamed the loudest scream I have EVER heard! And then he tried to stand up, but his body just went all wobbly, and he fell back down into his chair and started mumbling something and pointing to where Maisie was still pointing. And then he fainted on the desk.

And I had absolutely NO IDEA why Zach had just fainted on the desk, because he doesn't usually faint unless it has to do with peas, because he's terrified of peas.

And then Jodi started shouting, "MISS

JONES! MISS JONES!"

And I thought she was shouting because of Zach fainting, but then I saw that Jodi was pointing now too!

And Jodi must have been much better at pointing than Maisie and Zach were, because this time I saw EXACTLY what everyone was looking at, and so did the rest of the class. And everyone started screaming. Even Miss Jones! Because there was a huge RAT in our classroom!

Once we had been EVACUATED from the classroom, we were all sent to the gym hall with 6B.

And then all the other classes started coming into the gym hall too, and loads of the year ones were crying, and some of the year six girls were hugging each other, and it was basically just like a nightmare.

And then Mr Graves came on to the stage, and everyone went silent and stared at him. And I was panicking a bit because we were sat

RIGHT IN FRONT OF THE STAGE

because we had been the first ones to be evacuated.

And then Mr Graves said, "Good

afternoon, boys and girls. As you may have already heard, we appear to have had an incident with a poor little mouse in one of the classrooms."

And that's when Jodi whispered, "That definitely wasn't a mouse. It was huge!"

And she was right. And I knew that Mr Graves was probably just pretending that it had been a mouse, because he didn't want everyone to know about the vampire rats. And that the only reason he was calling the rat a "poor little mouse" was because it was probably one of his vampire friends, and he didn't want anyone to squish it.

And then all of a sudden Mr Graves looked right at us and froze. And his eyes went really wide. And that's when Maisie gasped and flopped on to my lap. But Mr Graves didn't even notice, so I knew it wasn't me or Maisie that he was staring at. So I turned and looked at Zach, and that's when I found out EXACTLY what Mr Graves was starting at. And I couldn't believe it. Zach's nose was bleeding!

So I screamed at the top of my lungs, **"ZACH! RUN!"** because I knew that Mr Graves was about to leap off the stage and drink Zach's nose blood!

But Zach didn't know that his nose was bleeding, so he didn't know what was going on, so he just sat there staring at me with his mouth wide open and blood all over his face.

And then Jodi grabbed Zach and covered his nose with her hand so Mr Graves couldn't see the blood.

And when we looked back at the stage, Mr Graves had gone really pale, and he was licking his lips! And then he started stumbling backwards, and he **WOULDN'T** take his eyes off Zach's nose, until he eventually turned and disappeared behind the curtain!

Once Mrs Seith had finished telling me off and giving me a detention for screaming during an assembly, she went on stage and quickly told everyone to collect a letter, and

that we were to give it to our parents, and that we were definitely **"NOT TO OPEN IT."** And then she told us to go outside for an extended afternoon interval until the end of the day, because of the mice that were really rats.

She didn't say **ANYTHING** about why Mr Graves had disappeared and I knew it was because she didn't know and that she was probably shocked, because all the other teachers had got in a group together at the bottom of the stage and they looked confused, and scared too, and they kept whispering to each other about it.

So as soon as Mrs Seith stopped talking I grabbed four letters and then we all ran out of the hall as fast as we could. And Jodi was in front, and she didn't stop running until she got to the very end of the playground, which is the furthest you can get from the Head Teacher's office. And then we all hid behind the recycling bins.

And then Jodi said, "I can't believe it. He almost got you!" And Zach looked like he was in shock.

And then I said that we had to get rid of all the nose blood so that Mr Graves wouldn't smell it and follow us. So I got my water bottle out and squeezed it all over Zach's face. But there was still loads of blood, and Jodi had it on her hands too from when she'd tried to cover Zach's face. And that's when Maisie opened her bag and she had LOADS of stuff, like antibacterial wipes, and plasters, and cotton wool, and she even had a big bandage.

So we used the antibacterial wipes on Jodi's hands and Zach's face so that Mr Graves DEFINITELY wouldn't be able to smell the blood and find us behind the recycling bins.

Then Zach said that his nose was really stinging now. And Maisie said that he must have hurt it when he fainted on the desk.

And then she said, "Izzy, you saved him." But I said that I didn't think I had because I'd told Zach to run but he'd just sat there.

But then Maisie said that Mr Graves had backed away because he knew that I had found out about him being a vampire because I'd screamed, "RUN!"

And then Zach said, "Do you think he's left for good?" And we all said that he might have, because he'd been found out.

And then I remembered about the letters, so I took mine out of my bag and opened it. And it said that there was a

"SLIGHT PEST ISSUE WITHIN THE SCHOOL"

and that certain areas of the school would be closed off until the situation was "FULLY RESOLVED". And that the school would remain open and that "LEARNING WOULD NOT BE AFFECTED".

And Maisie said that that wasn't really true, because she hadn't learned anything this week because all she could think about was rats and vampires.

And then Jodi said, "So should I still make garlic muffins tonight?"

And Zach said, "Um. Definitely!" And then he pointed up to the top corridor that was strictly **"OUT OF BOUNDS"**. And that's where we saw Mr Graves looking out of a window **RIGHT AT US.**

Garlic Muffins

The next day when me and Zach got to school, there was a sign up that said that all parts of the school were open again, except for the top corridor. But our classroom is on the top corridor, so that meant we were still sharing with 6B.

Zach said that the top corridor must be where all the rats had gathered, and that when we'd seen Mr Graves up there yesterday, he was probably feeding them all, and keeping them safe, and telling them all about how he nearly got to drink Zach's nose blood, and that all the rats would have been drooling because they wanted some.

And then I had an EPIPHANY. Which is when you realise something all of a sudden and it makes perfect sense. So I said, "Mr Murphy! They've got him!"

And Zach gasped, so I knew that he understood. So we ran to the new classroom,

and when we saw Jodi and Maisie waiting outside for us, we just shouted, **"DEN!"** and kept on running, and Jodi and Maisie ran after us.

Once we were in The Den, I told everyone about how I thought that Mr Graves had kidnapped Mr Murphy so that he could be the new Head Teacher and take over the school with his vampire-rat army. And about how poor Mr Murphy must be trapped up in the top corridor, and that he probably had hundreds of rat poos all over his face, and that he was probably really thirsty by now.

And then Zach said, "We need to save him for Miss Jones! She must be upset because she probably thinks that Mr Murphy just ran away and left her! She doesn't know about him being kidnapped and trapped by vampire rats!"

And then Jodi said, "Don't worry. We'll save him." And then she went into her bag and brought out an old ice-cream box.

And then she said, "Look." And she opened the lid, and showed us the garlic muffins. And

I was surprised, because I thought that they would stink, but they didn't. And then Jodi told us that she had chopped up the garlic and mixed it in with peanut butter, and put it right in the middle of the muffin, so that Mr Graves wouldn't smell it and get suspicious.

And then she said, "He'll just bite into the middle, and then it'll be too late."

And I thought that Jodi was probably a real-life genius, because this was the sneakiest and best plan

EVER.

At break time, we were getting ready to take the garlic muffin to Mr Graves when we realised that we had **NO IDEA** how we were going to actually get him to eat it.

Zach said that he thought we should just leave it outside his door, with a note. But then I said that I didn't think Mr Graves would just eat something that was left outside his door even if it did have a note on it. And that I didn't think **ANYONE** would just eat something they found sitting on the ground like that. But then Zach said that he would.

So I said, "But what if a dog had done his business on it? You wouldn't know, would

you?" And then Zach said that he'd changed his mind. And that he wouldn't eat a muffin off the ground. So we needed another plan.

So that's when Jodi said that there was only one way to make sure Mr Graves ate the muffin. And that it was for one of us to actually go up and knock on his door and give it to him. And everyone just kind of looked down at the ground, because none of us wanted to be the one to do it, and we were all just hoping that Jodi would say that she would do it.

But then Jodi said, "I'm not doing it. I made the muffin. It's someone else's turn."

And we all knew that she was right.

But then I remembered about yesterday, and how Maisie had said that Mr Graves had run away because he knew that I had found out about him being a vampire.

So I said, "I can't do it. He knows that I know about him!"

And then Zach said, "I'll do it." And we were all a bit shocked, because usually we have to force Zach into being brave and doing stuff. But then Zach looked at Maisie and smiled, and I knew that he had said that he would do it so that Maisie didn't have to.

So we watched from behind the big pot

plant in reception, as Zach went up to the new Head Teacher's door and knocked on it.

And then Jodi said, "Oh no. We didn't tell him what to say!"

And then she started panicking, and waving her arms about through the pot plant to try to get his attention, because we both knew that there was **NO WAY** Zach was going to be able to make up a story-lie about why he was giving the Head Teacher a muffin. And that he'd probably say something stupid like, "Have you been to another funeral today?" or "Do vampires eat muffins?!"

But then just as Zach noticed us, Mr Graves opened his door.

So I whispered, "Freeze!" And we did. But then I realised that that was a stupid plan, because our arms were still sticking out.

And then Mr Graves said, "Oh … erm … hello! Zachery, isn't it?"

And we heard Zach say, "Yes."

And then Mr Graves said, "Do those arms belong to you?"

And me and Jodi both pulled our arms back in right away!

And then Zach said, "Erm … yeah. That's my friends. They're shy."

And Mr Graves said, "Oh. I see."

I was impressed that Zach had thought to say that instead of saying something stupid like, "No, those are not my friends. That's just a plant with human arms."

And then Jodi whispered, "Izzy, open your eyes." And I didn't even realise that I'd had my eyes shut.

And that's when I saw Zach holding the garlic muffin up to Mr Graves.

And then he said, "We made this for you … to say welcome to our school."

It was hard to see what was going on because the pot plant was shaking like mad because Maisie was freaking out. But then I heard Mr Graves say thank you, and I moved a bit so I could see. And that's when I saw Mr Graves eat THE WHOLE THING.

And then he said, "That was delicious,

Zachery. Thank you. And your friends." And
then he looked right at the pot plant and
smiled a really, really
creepy smile!

Moth Jar Spy

When we got back to class, Jodi said that we needed to have an emergency meeting **RIGHT NOW** to discuss the **MUFFIN INCIDENT**. So we just pretended to be discussing our poems about nature and had a secret meeting instead.

Jodi said that she didn't understand why it hadn't worked, and that he'd eaten the **WHOLE MUFFIN**, and that she'd put at least **SIX** whole garlic cloves in it.

And then Zach said that something was wrong. And that there was **NO WAY** a vampire could eat that much garlic without exploding.

But then Miss Jones came over, and she just stood there, which is what she always does when she thinks we're chatting about things that are not our work. And then she said that we were just to carry on sharing our poems, and to pretend that she wasn't there.

And I didn't know **WHAT** to do, because none of us had written our poems, because we'd been having a secret meeting.

So I just said, "I like trees, but I don't like bees." And then I couldn't think of anything else to say, so I just STARED at Jodi, and tried to kick her a bit under the table. And then Jodi said, "Grass is green, and so is a bean."

And then we both stared at Zach, and he started saying all this stuff about how nature was beautiful and special and that nature was all around us, and then he started talking about baby animals, and even though it wasn't really a poem, and it didn't rhyme or anything, Miss Jones seemed really happy about what Zach had said, and that made her go away.

Then Maisie said something, but we couldn't really hear what it was because she had both of her pigtails in her mouth,

because she sometimes eats her hair when she's scared. So we asked her to take them out, and she did.

And then she said, "I think Mr Graves knew that we'd put garlic in the muffin." And then she said that the way he had eaten ALL of it RIGHT IN FRONT OF US and then smiled RIGHT AT US afterwards made her think that he KNEW what we were up to. And that he knew that nothing was going to happen to him.

And then Miss Jones came back over to our table and separated us for not doing our work.

At lunch, we went to The Den to finish the secret meeting.

We were all still really confused about how Mr Graves could have known about our plan, because we'd made it in secret, in The Den. And we hadn't told anyone else about it.

So I said, "But how did he find out? Who told him?"

And that's when Jodi paused, and her eyes went a bit wide.

And then she whispered, "We did." And we were all shocked that she'd said that.

And I said, "What?! No we never!"

Then Jodi whispered, "DON'T freak out. I want everyone to stay very, very calm."

And that's when Maisie started shaking VIOLENTLY.

And Zach started saying, "What? WHAT?!" And NOBODY was being calm, because we all knew that something was SERIOUSLY WRONG because people ALWAYS tell you to STAY CALM when things are SERIOUSLY WRONG. I don't know why they even bother saying it because it just makes everyone PANIC!

Then Jodi started acting REALLY weird, and smiling loads.

And then she said, "I think I'll draw a picture of the four of us for the moth. We can put it up there beside its jar."

And I didn't know **WHAT** was going on, because the moth died **AGES** ago, when we fed it cheese by mistake, so I didn't know what Jodi was talking about.

And then Jodi got her notepad out of her bag and started drawing. And she was acting all happy and whistling while she was doing it, and she looked completely **CRAZY**.

And then she said, "Izzy, come and see. Doesn't this drawing look exactly like you?"

So I looked at Zach. And I knew that we were both thinking the same thing, and that it was that Jodi was having her mind controlled. But when I looked up at Jodi

again, she widened her eyes a bit, just for a second, and that made me think that it was a SECRET SIGNAL, and that maybe Jodi WASN'T having her mind controlled.

So I went over to her and looked at the drawing. But she hadn't drawn anything. She had WRITTEN something in big letters. And it said:

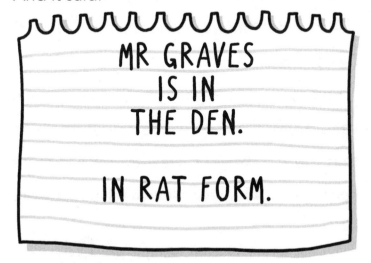

MR GRAVES
IS IN
THE DEN.

IN RAT FORM.

I gasped a bit when I read it. And that made Jodi start laughing really loud, but it wasn't her normal laugh.

Then she said, "My drawing of you isn't **THAT** bad, Izzy!"

And I knew right there and then that Jodi definitely **WASN'T** having her mind controlled, and that she was just **ACTING** because Rat Mr Graves was in here **SPYING** on us!

And so even though my hand was shaking, I grabbed the notebook and pen. And then I said, "Erm … you should draw my hair more like this." But I didn't draw any hair. I wrote:

WHERE?!
WHAT DO WE DO??!

And then Jodi said, "OK," and she pretended that she was fixing my hair, but instead she wrote:

ON THE SHELF
WHERE THE MOTH
USED TO LIVE!
KEEP QUIET
OR HE'LL POUNCE!

And I looked up at the shelf and saw him. And I must have gasped again, because all of a sudden Jodi started singing really loudly and clapping her hands. So I just joined in, because I knew Jodi was trying to cover up the fact that I'd gasped again, so that we could pretend to Mr Graves that we didn't know he was on the shelf watching us.

And then Zach said, "What's going on?!"

And just then the bell rang, and Jodi jumped up and said, "Wow! Yes! Time for class. Let's go!" And she started half-skipping, half-running out of the door. And we all followed her.

As soon as we were in the classroom, and Miss Jones was doing the register, we told Zach and Maisie what had **REALLY** been going on in The Den.

Zach looked a bit sick.

And Maisie squealed, "**WHAT?** Why didn't you tell us?!" And I knew that the reason Jodi had told only me, and not Maisie or Zach, was because I was the only one brave enough to handle it.

So I took Maisie's hand and told her that everything was OK and that if Mr Graves had moved even one rat muscle I would have got her out of there

And she nodded like she believed me, but she kept shaking anyway.

And then Jodi said that when Maisie had been talking, she had seen something move on the shelf beside the old moth jar. And that it had been a rat, and that she had looked right into its eyes, and that she just KNEW it was Mr Graves.

Then Jodi said, "He must have been there when we made the garlic-muffin plan. That's how he knew what we were up to! We told him!"

And then Zach said that she was right, and that he probably took some sort of garlic protection potion so that he could eat garlic without it harming him.

And that's when we all became very **PARANOID**. And we kept checking under the table, and in the pen pot, and in our bags in case Mr Graves or one of his vampire army were spying on us.

And then Zach whispered, "I know what we have to do."

Dogs, Rabies and Recycling Bins

As soon as the bell went for lunch, we all looked at Zach. And he said, "Follow me." So we did.

Zach got in line with the rest of the class to go to the dinner hall, like we always do. But then when we got to the bottom of the stairs, and Miss Jones turned right to go into the dinner hall, Zach turned left and started running along the bottom corridor and out through the Big Doors. So we ran after him, and we kept running until we got to the

grassy bit, because Zach stopped.

Then Zach said that we needed to check that Mr Graves wasn't in rat-form, hiding in the long grass, before he told us about his plan. So I said that we should go over to the flat concrete bit, because there was no way a rat could hide on the flat concrete bit without us noticing. So that's what we did.

And that's when Zach said that it was time to do something more serious. Because we'd tried the garlic muffin, and that hadn't worked. And that even though Mr Graves KNEW that WE KNEW about him being a vampire, he was still here, which meant that

he was still planning to ATTACK with his vampire-rat army. And that we had to do something before they took over the school and drank everyone's blood.

And then Maisie said, "Do you think they're going to turn us into vampires too?"

And Jodi said that they might, to make their army stronger.

But then Zach said, "It doesn't matter what their plan is, because in about five minutes Mr Graves will be DUST!"

So we all went really quiet and listened, because we really wanted Mr Graves to be dust, and we knew we only had five minutes to do Zach's plan.

Then Zach said, "We're going to force Mr Graves to come outside into the sunlight, and then he'll turn to DUST!"

And I thought that that was a

BRILLIANT IDEA

because we hadn't actually seen Mr Graves outside in the playground, not even ONCE, even though Mr Murphy ALWAYS used to be outside keeping an eye on us, in case we were doing VANDALISM or digging a pool for seals to live in.

And then Zach said that it was going to take something BIG to force Mr Graves to come outside. And that the plan was to pretend that there was a SERIOUS INCIDENT happening in the playground, and that it was that two big dogs with rabies had got into the school, and that they were fighting TO THE DEATH beside the recycling bins, and that Maisie was trapped inside one of the recycling bins, because she'd hidden in there when the dogs had run into the playground.

And then he said, "We have to make sure that the office ladies know too, so that if

Mr Graves refuses to come outside and save Maisie's life, everyone will know. And Mr Graves will get sacked, because Head Teachers aren't allowed to let pupils stay trapped inside a recycling bin that's next to two dogs with rabies."

And then Jodi said that it was a perfect plan. And we all agreed. And I was a bit jealous that I hadn't been the one who thought of it because it really **WAS** perfect. Because even if we couldn't get Mr Graves to come outside and turn to dust, we'd still be able to get rid of him because he'd be sacked from being the new Head Teacher if he didn't come out.

So me and Jodi and Zach told Maisie to stay hidden in the recycling bin, and to make sure she kept the lid open a bit, so she could

breathe, and then we ran back towards the school.

When we got to the Big Doors, Jodi said that we had to make it look like there really **WERE** big dogs with rabies in the school trying to attack Maisie. And that we should probably all be crying, and that our hair should be all over the place. So we all opened our eyes really wide and used our hands to fan air into them until our eyes started watering, and there were tears running down our faces. And then we made our hair all messy.

Then Jodi said, "As soon as I open this

door, start screaming as loud as you can, OK?" And we said OK. And then Jodi counted to three and opened the door.

He's
Burning!

As soon as the door was open we all started screaming and running down the corridor until we got to the Head Teacher's office.

When we got there, there were already loads of teachers who had come running out of their classrooms, and all the office ladies ran up to the glass window. But the Head Teacher wasn't there. And his door was still shut.

And that's when I looked at Jodi. And that's when I decided to be brave. So I ran right up to the Head Teacher's door, opened it and went in.

Even though it was really dark inside, I could still kind of see Mr Graves sitting at his desk. So I started screaming all about Maisie and the rabies dogs, and then I ran right out again. And then me and Jodi and Zach shouted, "Follow us! FOLLOW US!" and we ran right along the corridor and outside

again, and even though all the teachers were shouting, **"STOP! COME BACK!"** we didn't, because we needed them to follow us.

But then when we got to the Big Doors, and we were almost outside, we heard Zach screaming for real. I was scared to turn around in case he was screaming because Mr Graves has bitten him in the neck, but when I did turn around I saw that he had fallen and hurt his leg.

So I went to go back for him. But then Zach shouted, "**NO!** You have to keep going! Mr Graves **NEEDS** to follow you!"

And Jodi said, "Izzy! He's right, let's go!

Come on!"

But I said, "No! What if there's blood on his knee? Mr Graves might get him!"

So we ran back to get Zach as quickly as we could, and dragged him out into the playground so he would be safe, in the sunlight.

Then as soon as we got to the recycling bins, we stopped and looked back to see if our plan had worked. We watched as Miss Jones, and then Miss Ross, and then Mr Killington, and then all of the office ladies came running outside. But Mr Graves wasn't there.

Then Zach said, "He's not coming."

And JUST as he said that the Big Doors burst open and Mr Graves came running out with a mop in his hand. And Zach panicked and jumped in the bin with Maisie because Mr Graves was running right towards us!

But then I noticed that Mr Graves was running a bit funny, kind of like side to side, instead of forward. And then when he eventually got a bit closer, I shouted, "LOOK!" and Maisie and Zach peeked out from the bin.

And then Jodi screamed, "His face! It's BURNING!!"

And it was! It was all red and covered in blotches and blisters! And so were his hands! And that's when Jodi shouted,

"HE'S MELTING! RUN!"

And Maisie and Zach both jumped right out of the bin and we all ran for our lives.

MEGA
Trouble

When we ran away from Mr Graves, we
didn't really know where to go, so we ran
right around to the other side of the school
and hid in the bush in the front car park. And
then we just sat there for ten whole minutes
trying to catch our breath, and calm down.

And that's when we heard the ambulance coming.

And Jodi said, "It's for Mr Graves!"

And Zach said, "There won't be anything left by the time they get here! He'll be dust!"

Then when the ambulance arrived, we watched as Miss Jones and one of the office ladies came rushing out of the front door holding Mr Graves by an arm each. And then they helped him into the ambulance.

And we all gasped when we saw them.

And then Jodi said, "Look how red his face is! It's almost completely melted!"

And Zach said that we must have got

it wrong, and that maybe it takes ages for vampires to actually burn completely and turn to dust in the sunlight.

And that's when I realised what had happened.

So I said, "It's not sunny enough." And everyone agreed that I was right, because it was a bit cold and it looked like it was about to start raining.

When the ambulance went away, we came out of the bush, because we didn't really have any other choice. And that's when Miss Jones came running over, and she hugged Maisie for ages, and then she said, "Thank

goodness! Are you OK?!"

Then the other teachers came rushing over too and they were all asking about the dogs. And that's when Zach TOTALLY got us into MEGA trouble because he started crying and told Miss Jones that he'd made it all up because the new Head Teacher was a vampire rat.

So we had no choice but to go back to the classroom and

tell Miss Jones EVERYTHING. And when we got to the bit about Mr Murphy being trapped on the top corridor with hundreds of rat poos all over his face, she just burst out laughing and said, "I wish!" and then she looked a bit embarrassed that she'd said it.

And that's when Miss Jones told us that Mr Murphy HAD left, and that he'd taken something called a CAREER BREAK, and that he'd gone to India to FIND HIMSELF. And then she said that he'd be back in six months.

And then she said that she didn't mean what she'd said about wishing Mr Murphy

was trapped with hundreds of rat poos, and that it hadn't been a very nice thing to say. But I don't think she meant it.

I didn't really believe that Mr Murphy had gone to FIND HIMSELF in India, because it didn't even make sense, and it was probably just what Mr Graves wrote in a letter to Miss Jones when he kidnapped Mr Murphy, so that Miss Jones wouldn't phone the police and report Mr Murphy as a missing person.

And then Zach said, "Are you and Mr Murphy still getting married when he gets back from India?"

And Miss Jones took a deep breath. And

then she said, "We'll see."

And that's when I knew that the reason Miss Jones was angry was because she thought that Mr Murphy had gone on holiday without her. Like the time Mum and Dad went on holiday to Spain, and I had to stay with Gran, and I was mad at them for ages because they didn't take me with them.

So anyway, we starting telling her about everything else that had happened, and when we got to the bit about making the garlic muffins, Miss Jones covered her mouth with her hands and said, "Oh NO! It was YOU!"

Then she started shaking her head, and then she grabbed her phone.

And that's when Maisie screamed,

"PLEASE!
PLEASE
MISS JONES!
DON'T PHONE
THE POLICE!
I DON'T WANT
TO GO
TO JAIL!"

And Miss Jones looked shocked. She covered the phone with her hand and told Maisie that it was OK, and that she definitely wasn't phoning the police, and that she was phoning the hospital to tell them about the GARLIC so they could help Mr Graves.

And then someone must have answered, because Miss Jones said, "Hello, is this Ward Eight? I'm calling regarding Stewart Graves."

And we all looked at each other because Miss Jones had said that Mr Graves's first name was Stewart.

And then Miss Jones said, "Can you

please let the doctor know that Stewart has DEFINITELY been exposed to garlic." And then Miss Jones listened for a bit. And then she covered the phone with her hand again and looked right at me and said, "Izzy, how much garlic did you give Mr Graves?"

So I pointed to Jodi. And Jodi said, "Six cloves." And Miss Jones rolled her eyes and shook her head, and then she told whoever she was speaking to that Mr Graves had INGESTED six cloves of garlic. And then she hung up, and just looked at us for ages. And she looked very cross.

Then she eventually said, "I suppose you

weren't to know this, but Mr Graves has a very serious GARLIC ALLERGY."

And then Jodi said, "We know that. ALL vampires have a serious garlic allergy."

And then Miss Jones sighed and put her head in her hands for a minute.

Then she said, "Listen VERY closely. Mr Graves is NOT a vampire. But he DOES have a lot of allergies. And garlic is one of them. That's why garlic has been banned from school dinners. It makes Mr Graves seriously ill if he comes into contact with garlic. That's why his skin looked so red and painful."

And we were all a bit shocked, because we

couldn't believe what we were hearing.

Then Miss Jones gave us a big lecture about hiding things in cakes and then giving them to people, and that we should never EVER do anything like that EVER AGAIN! And then she made us put the leftover garlic muffins in the bin.

Then Miss Jones said that when the Head Teacher was feeling better and came back to school, that she'd have to tell him what we did, and that we'd have to apologise.

Sorry For Melting Your Face

On Monday, we went to class early, like Miss Jones had asked us to do. That's when she told us that Mr Graves was back, and that he was waiting to see all four of us in his office, and that we should go down and apologise to him right away, even before registration.

And that we should mean it.

But then just as we were about to go down, Miss Jones called us back. And she started walking around us and sniffing us, like a dog. And then she said, "Oh my goodness! Do I smell GARLIC?!"

And I looked around to see if Jodi had brought another garlic muffin with her, but she looked just as surprised as I was that Miss Jones thought we had garlic. And that's when I saw Maisie's face. And Maisie was looking a bit guilty, and I knew that it was probably because she was hiding garlic in her pocket or her bag or something because she was terrified of vampires.

So I just said, "No, Miss Jones. We've not got garlic. I just had lasagne and garlic bread for my tea last night, that's all." Because I didn't want Maisie to get told off.

Miss Jones looked at us for a bit.

And then she said, "Fine. Well, I think you'd all better just leave your coats and bags here before you go down. And perhaps you should just empty your pockets too. Thank you."

But me and Jodi and Maisie didn't have any pockets. So we just watched as Zach emptied his.

And then Miss Jones said, "OK, off you go. And PLEASE make sure you apologise properly. What you did was very serious."

And it made me feel really bad when Miss Jones said that, because if Mr Graves really wasn't a vampire rat and just a normal human Head Teacher who was allergic to garlic, then what we did to him wasn't very nice, and his skin must've been really sore. Like the time before Mum found out I was allergic to plasters, and she put a plaster on my elbow, and it got so itchy that I scratched it all night in my sleep. And then in the morning it was so sore, and red, and blistery that I thought I was maybe going to die.

So anyway, we all said that we would apologise to Mr Graves properly, and then we left.

⭐

It took AGES to get Maisie down the stairs to the Head Teacher's office. And every time we got down three or four of the stairs, Maisie would just go all wobbly again and have to sit down for a bit.

And in the end, Jodi had to carry Maisie on her back, even though it is completely against the school rules to give piggy-backs ever since Finola Burke tried to give Roz Morgan a piggy-back, even though Roz Morgan was already giving Andrew Cunningham a piggy-back at the time, and then they all fell on top of Mrs Kidd in the playground.

Anyway, when we got to the Head Teacher's office, we just stood outside the door because none of us wanted to be the one to knock.

And that's when we overheard the office ladies talking about Mr Graves, and how sore his face had looked. But then one of them starting talking about a PADLOCK, but we couldn't really hear everything they were saying, because they were whispering. And then another one said, "And it's always so dark in there. He's a bit strange, isn't he?"

and me and Jodi looked RIGHT at each other, because we both knew that the MIND CONTROL must be wearing off!

But then one of the office ladies spotted us, and she looked at us like we were muffin hooligans or something! And then she shook her head and said, "Wait there!" and then pointed to the Time Out chairs.

So we were just about to sit down and wait, when Mr Graves opened his door. And we were all shocked! Because all of his blotches and blisters were gone!

Then Mr Graves said, "In you come then, have a seat." And I noticed that his voice

didn't sound as scary as it usually does.

So we all went inside and sat down. And all the blinds and curtains were open, and it wasn't dark at all.

We all STARED at Mr Graves as he sat down at his desk. And then we watched as he took out a tube of cream and rubbed some on his hands. And that's when I noticed that his hands were still a bit red and sore, and I felt really guilty.

Then Mr Graves said, "So … Miss Jones tells me we have our very own Vampire Hunters in the school. Is that right?" And then he started smiling. And I noticed that

he didn't have any fangs.

I looked at Jodi, because I didn't know what to say, but she was just looking down at the ground, and so were Zach and Maisie. So I said, "Yes, that's right."

And Mr Graves said, "And is it true that you think I'M a vampire?"

But I didn't say anything this time; I just nodded and looked down at the ground like everyone else was doing, because I'd already said something.

And then Mr Graves burst out LAUGHING! And it didn't sound creepy like I thought it would when a vampire laughed, it sounded

SILLY! And his nose kept making this weird snorty sound.

We all just STARED at him until he eventually stopped and dried his eyes with a tissue and said, "I'm sorry, but I just think that's the FUNNIEST thing I've ever heard in my LIFE! I'd be the worst vampire in the world. I'm absolutely

of the sight of blood!"

And that's when we all looked at each other, because we realised that that must've been the reason why Mr Graves acted so weird when he saw Zach's nose blood; he was scared!

And then Mr Graves said, "I must ask. Why on EARTH would you think that I was a vampire?!"

So I looked at Jodi. But Jodi just did her WIDE EYES at me, which meant that she wanted ME to be the one who told Mr Graves why we thought he was a vampire. But I didn't think that was very fair, because I had already answered two of Mr Graves's

questions, and Jodi hadn't answered ANY,
so I just did even WIDER eyes back at her

until she eventually said, "There were lots of
reasons."

And Mr Graves said, "There WERE?!" and

then he started laughing again. And I was starting to think that we had **DEFINTELY** got it wrong, because Mr Graves seemed really surprised that anyone would think he was a vampire, and because I didn't think he really looked like a vampire any more. And also because I didn't think a vampire would have such a silly, snorty laugh.

So then Jodi pointed to the creepy cape photo on the wall.

And she said, "Why are you wearing a cape in that photo?"

And Mr Graves said, **"CAPE?"** And then he turned around and looked at the photo

and said, "Oh, I see. You thought that was a vampire's cape. Well, that is actually a TEACHER'S GOWN. The first school I taught in was a very traditional school. All of the teachers had to wear them. And they were very itchy!" And then he smiled at us.

And then Zach said, "I bet you're glad you don't have to wear one of those at this school." And I couldn't BELIEVE that Zach was saying stuff like that when we were supposed to be saying sorry for melting Mr Graves's face!

And Mr Graves said, "Oh yes, I'm very pleased. I really like it here!"

And that made me feel even MORE guilty when he said that, because Mr Graves really liked it here, even though his pupils had tried to turn him to dust with a garlic muffin!

And then Jodi explained that one of the other reasons we thought he was a vampire was because he had lots of creepy old furniture from Olden Times.

And Mr Graves said, "These are ANTIQUES, Jodi. They are very special!" And then he got a bit excited and started telling us this LONG and BORING story about the head-with-a-bit-of-shoulders-but-no-body statue on his desk, which I think he called a BUST, but I'm not sure, because it was really boring, so I couldn't listen to all of it.

And then once he had finished his story, he showed us even MORE antiques that

were in his drawer, and then he asked me if I liked them. And I didn't. But I didn't want to say that and hurt his feelings because

we'd already hurt his skin, and I didn't want to lie either, and I was a hundred per cent convinced that Mr Graves wasn't a vampire now because we hadn't read anywhere that vampires were this boring, so I just said, "I'm really sorry we melted your face, Mr Graves." And I meant it.

And Mr Graves said, "I forgive you. You weren't to know that I was allergic to garlic. I really shouldn't have just eaten the muffin without checking what was in it first. But I was just so pleased that you had made it for me. It was such a nice way to welcome me to your school. I must admit, I was a little

nervous that no one would like me. I hear Mr Murphy was very popular!"

And we all STARED at each other, because we were a bit shocked that Mr Graves had been so nervous, and that he had been worrying that we wouldn't like him. And also because we didn't really think that Mr Murphy had been very popular.

And that's when Jodi and Zach and Maisie all said sorry too. And Mr Graves said, "Thank you."

And then Zach said, "So it really is MICE in the school then, not vampire rats?"

And I thought Mr Graves was going to

burst out laughing, because if he thought vampires were so funny, then he would definitely think VAMPIRE RATS were funny!

But he didn't laugh, he looked a bit nervous.

And then he said, "Yes … erm … just one or two little mice. But we'll catch them soon, and then they'll be rehomed. Don't worry."

And that's when Jodi said, "There weren't any leaks in the roof, were there? You just didn't want to tell us that there were mice in the school."

And Mr Graves said, "Yes, you're right. I'm sorry. We didn't want to cause a panic."

And then Jodi said that she forgave him for the leak lie, and that made him smile again, but he still looked a bit weird in the face.

And that's when I remembered something. Something that hadn't been explained yet.

So I said, "Mr Graves, why did we hear hissing coming from your room?"

And Mr Graves stopped smiling.

And he said, "Hissing? I … I have no idea. How strange. Are you sure?"

And then Jodi said that she'd heard it too.

And then Mr Graves said, "Oh, I know! It must've been when I was pumping up my bike tyres. That's it. No vampires hissing in here! Ha, ha." And then he started smiling again, but it didn't look like when he had smiled before.

And then he got up really quickly and said, "OK, let's get you all back to class."

So we got up and started walking towards the door, and that's when Maisie pointed to where the big folded-up box that had said FRAGILE had been.

And then she said, "What was in the big long box we saw, Mr Graves?"

And Mr Graves froze, and his face started to go a bit red.

And then he eventually said, "Erm …

just my books. But I'm all unpacked now as you can see." And then he pointed to his bookcase, and we looked and saw that there were hardly ANY books in it!

And then Mr Graves opened the door and said, "Um. You must excuse me; I have to make a call. Good day."

So we all said, "Good day," back, except for Maisie, because she'd already run out the door!

Who
Hissed?!

Maisie must have run REALLY fast back to the classroom, because we all ran after her our fastest, but by the time we got back up to the classroom, Maisie was already sitting down at the table searching in her bag.

So we all went up to Miss Jones and quickly

told her that we'd apologised, and that Mr Graves had accepted our apology. But we didn't mention anything about the box and the hissing, or about how weird Mr Graves had acted when we asked about them, or about how we were sure he was a vampire again.

Then when we got back to our table, Maisie had something on around her neck. And it was a garlic necklace. And it was stinking.

And then Jodi said, "Maisie! Hide that! Miss Jones will go mad!"

So Maisie tucked the smelly necklace inside her shirt.

Then she said, "Did you see his face when I asked about the box?"

And we nodded.

And Maisie said, "Do you know what I think was in that box?"

And we all looked at each other and nodded again, because we knew.

And that's when Maisie opened her pencil case and took out another three garlic necklaces. And we all took them and put

them on right away. Because we all knew that what had been in the box was Mr Graves's COFFIN!

At break, we went to the school reception and hid behind the pot plant, because that was the plan. We were going to prove once and for all that Mr Graves WAS a vampire with a vampire-rat army, and that he wanted to drink our blood and take over the school.

We knew what we had to do. We needed to break into Mr Graves's office, find his coffin, take a photo of it with Zach's mobile phone, and then show it to Miss Jones so that she

would believe us and phone the police, or the government, or the real army. That was our only option.

So we waited until the office ladies weren't looking, and we ran across the reception and sneaked into the Head Teacher's office. I was a bit scared that Mr Graves was actually going to be in there when we sneaked in, but he wasn't. And Jodi had said that he wouldn't be, because she said that ALL the teachers DEFINITELY go to the staff room at morning break, and that it was a RULE if you were a teacher, so all the teachers had to go, even the head.

So as soon as we got in, we started searching for a secret passageway, or a trap door, that led to where Mr Graves kept the coffin that he slept in. But we couldn't find anything.

And then Maisie pointed to the cupboard door. And I'd never really thought about the coffin being in a cupboard, because I just thought it would be somewhere more secret than that, like down a set of secret stairs under Mr Graves's big desk. But this was no ordinary cupboard. There was something very suspicious about this cupboard. It had a PADLOCK on it! And that's when we realised

that it must be the same padlock that the office ladies had been gossiping about!

Then Zach said, "That's it! That's where he keeps it!"

And then I said that we needed to find the key, and

QUICK,

before he came back and caught us.

So we started opening all the drawers and searching for the key, but we couldn't find it anywhere, and then Jodi said, "Look!" and she held up a set of CAR KEYS.

And then she said, "He doesn't have a BIKE! He drives a CAR to school!"

And that's when I noticed a tiny little key hanging on the key chain.

So I grabbed the keys out of Jodi's hand and ran over to the cupboard and put it in the padlock. And it worked!

But then Zach said, "What if he's in there? Sleeping?"

And we all thought about that for a moment. But then Jodi just grabbed the handle and pulled down really hard and fast before we could do anything. And the door opened.

It was so dark inside the cupboard that we really couldn't see anything.

And then Zach said, "Find the light." But we couldn't, so we had to walk inside a bit and feel our way around, and it felt like a REALLY BIG cupboard, because even

though I was putting both of my arms out, I couldn't feel anything.

And then we all heard it at the same time. Hissing!

And Jodi started screaming, "He's in the coffin! HE'S IN THE COFFIN! GET OUT! GET OUT!" But it was too dark, and I tried to get out, but both me and Zach tripped on Maisie, who was lying on the ground because she'd fainted. And then the hissing started to get even louder, and I reached out to grab Jodi and felt the light switch on the wall, and Zach was screaming and crying for his mum, so I just hit the light switch, and that's when

we saw the giant

Mary

We all just stood there screaming and staring at the giant snake! And then we all kind of realised at the same time that the snake was trapped in a glass tank, and that we probably weren't going to die.

And then Jodi said, "Is that MR GRAVES?!"

And me and Zach didn't know **WHAT** to
say, and Maisie was still out cold on the floor.
And then we heard another
scream, and we turned

around and
saw Mr Graves
standing in the doorway!

And he said, "Oh no! You found Mary!"

And I gasped and jumped a bit when he
said it, because I thought that maybe there
was **ANOTHER** vampire in the cupboard, a

lady one, called Mary. But then Mr Graves ran over to the giant snake and put his hand in the tank and said, "Ssssh, Mary. There, there. Did you get a little fright, my beautiful lady?"

And Jodi's mouth was hanging wide open, because she was probably shocked that the giant snake was called Mary, and also because there even WAS a giant snake in the new Head Teacher's cupboard!

And then the snake stopped hissing, and kind of curled up in the corner of its huge tank and went to sleep.

And then Maisie started to wake up, so we grabbed her and got her out of the cupboard as quickly as possible, because we didn't want her to see Mary.

Then Mr Graves put out the cupboard light and shut the door.

And then he said, "I'm sorry. I hope Mary didn't scare you. I owe you an explanation."

And we all just stared at him, because we didn't know **WHAT** he was going to say. And that's when Mr Graves told us that Mary was his pet. And that he'd had her for over ten years. And that he couldn't keep Mary at his house any more, because his fiancée had come to live with him, and she was terrified of snakes.

And then he looked really sad, and a bit like he was going to start crying.

And that's when I realised that it had been MARY we'd heard hissing when we were standing outside Mr Graves's office. And that MARY was the beautiful lady Mr Graves had been talking to!

"She really is a wonderful snake," said Mr Graves. "She didn't mean any harm when

she hissed at you like that. She just doesn't like the strong light, you see."

And then he started biting his nails, like Mum does when she's scared or nervous about something. And I knew that Mr Graves was probably biting his nails because he was worried that we were going to tell someone and that he was going to get into

for having a **SNAKE** in the school.

So we all looked at each other, and I felt really bad for Mr Graves, and for Mary,

because they obviously loved each other, and it wasn't fair what was happening to them. And the only reason Mr Graves had lied to us was because he was trying to protect Mary.

So I said, "You should just keep her here, in your cupboard. We won't tell anyone."

But Mr Graves said that he would get into

BIG TROUBLE

if the council found out that Mary was on school premises, and that she couldn't stay here any longer.

And then Zach said, "I'll take her."

And that must've cheered Mr Graves up, because he smiled and laughed a bit.

And then he said, "Thanks, Zach. But Mary has already been adopted. Someone who keeps exotic animals is coming to collect her early tomorrow morning."

And I felt so sad for Mr Graves, because if Mum or Dad ever said to me that they were terrified of our two cats, and that we had to put them up for adoption, I would

definitely cry forever. And then I'd probably just take the cats and move into Zach's house downstairs.

So that's when we knew for sure that Mr Graves wasn't a vampire. And that he was just a Head Teacher who was allergic to garlic and kept a giant snake called Mary in his cupboard.

So before we all left to go to class, we told Mr Graves that we wouldn't tell

ANYONE

about Mary. And that we were sorry he had

to give her up. And Mr Graves said thank you. And we said that it was OK, and we said thank you again to him too, for forgiving us about the garlic muffin.

But then Maisie said, "Mr Graves…" And we all got a bit of a surprise, because we thought Maisie would be too scared to talk after hearing all about Mary, but she wasn't.

And then she said, "Mary is a very large snake. What does she eat?"

And Mr Graves's cheeks went a bit pink again, and I was scared it was because he was about to say that Mary drank blood!

But then Mr Graves said, "Err, well, she

eats lots of things, actually."

And then Maisie said, "Does she eat mice?"

And Mr Graves's cheeks went even REDDER.

And he said, "Yes."

And then Maisie whispered, "Live mice?"

And Mr Graves nodded, and looked down at the ground.

And we were all **SHOCKED**, because Mary ate **LIVE MICE** (which is horrible!) and that meant that she kind of **WAS** a vampire.

And that's when we realised why there were mice loose in our school. Mary's dinner had escaped!

We Love
You Scary
Mary

When we got to school the next day, all of the DANGER! KEEP OUT! signs were gone, and we were allowed to go back to our old classroom again.

I was pleased that the signs were down because that meant that we didn't have to

share a classroom with 6B any more, and it also meant that the mice must be gone. And I hoped that they'd been found and adopted, like Mary had. And that they hadn't been given to Scary Mary for her tea!

At break time, we all went to The Den to do a new plan. Jodi had brought all of her glitter pens, and she'd even brought the pink one, which she only brings out on really, really special occasions, like this. And Zach had printed out the photo he had taken. And Maisie had brought a frame from her house.

Once we were finished, Jodi said, "What do you think?"

And I said that I thought it was probably the most beautiful picture I had ever seen, even though it **WAS** a photo of a scary-looking giant snake with **"MARY"** written in glitter on it.

Then when we were leaving The Den, we saw **MR MURPHY!** And he was wearing **JEANS** and a beaded **NECKLACE** and he was **RUNNING** along the corridor, and he had the **BIGGEST TEDDY I'VE EVER SEEN!**

So we followed him.

And he ran right into our classroom and picked Miss Jones up off her seat and gave her a big hug! And she looked SHOCKED. And we all knew it was because she was probably wondering why Mr Murphy was here instead of being all the way in India.

And I was just about to ask Mr Murphy if he was coming back to be our Head Teacher again, and if we could please see the giant teddy, when Miss Jones gave Mr Murphy a BIG KISS!

And Zach started cheering and clapping, even though it was disgusting, and that's when Miss Jones laughed, and then she picked up the giant teddy and sat it on her desk. And we all laughed and ran away.

We ran all the way to Mr Graves's office, because we were too excited to walk, because of the giant teddy and also because we couldn't WAIT to show Mr Graves what we'd made for him!

And when we got there we were also too excited to knock, so we just kind of all rushed in.

Mr Graves was sitting at his desk. And when he saw us he smiled a bit and said, "Oh, hello!" And he said it in a way that I knew meant he was trying to sound cheerful,

but that he wasn't really feeling very cheerful because he missed Mary.

So we all walked up to his desk and gave him the picture of Mary in the frame. And he looked VERY surprised. And it was probably because he wasn't expecting to ever see Mary ever again and also because he didn't know that we had sneaked back into his office again at lunchtime and used Zach's mobile phone to take a picture of Mary.

Then Mr Graves smiled loads and said, "Thank you. This is very special." And I didn't think that his lips looked anything like worms any more. They looked a bit like normal lips,

but not completely.

And then Mr Graves took down the scary cape picture and put the picture that WE'D made up on the wall!

And then the bell went so I said, "Good day, Mr Graves."

And Mr Graves laughed a bit and said, "Good day, Izzy."

And it was brilliant.

Acknowledgements

A big THANK YOU to Thomas for bringing Izzy and the gang to life. You are fantastic!

Thanks also to the amazing Kirsty, brilliant Nicola, and all of the very fabulous team at Nosy Crow.

And (of course) thanks to my husband, Andy, who likes to remind me that HE helped come up with the "vampire thing" on the train that day.